MOLLY AND EMMETT'S
Camping Adventure

Marylin Hafner

Cricket/McGraw-Hill

"Molly and Emmett" appears monthly in *Ladybug*® magazine.
Visit our Web site at www.ladybugmag.com or call 1-800-827-0227
or write to *Ladybug* magazine, 315 Fifth Street, Peru, IL 61354.

Send all inquiries to:
McGraw-Hill Consumer Products
8787 Orion Place
Columbus, OH 43240-4027

1-57768-894-5

1 2 3 4 5 6 7 8 9 10 RRD-W 05 04 03 02 01 00

Library of Congress Cataloging-in-Publication Data

Hafner, Marylin.
  Molly and Emmett's camping adventure / Marylin Hafner.
    p. cm.
  Summary: When Molly and her cat Emmett find an old tent in the
basement, they set up camp in the backyard, but the weather changes
their plans. Includes activity ideas for backyard camping.
  ISBN 1-57768-894-5
  [1. Cats–Fiction. 2. Camping–Fiction.]   I. Title.
  PZ7.H1225 Mo 2000
  [E]–dc21
                                        00-010029

One day when they found themselves with nothing to do, Molly and Emmett decided to explore the basement.

They discovered wonderful surprises . . . boxes and bundles of all shapes and sizes.

Emmett found his favorite blue fish pillow. He thought he'd lost it a long time ago.

Molly found some camping equipment.
It gave her a wonderful idea.

"Let's camp out tonight, Emmett!" she said.

But Emmett had already looked outside.

"I think it's going to rain, Molly," he said.

"Trust me, Em," said Molly. "It'll be fun. We'll be
dry and cozy inside our tent. C'mon!"

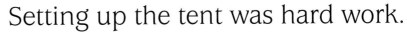

Setting up the tent was hard work.

Finally the tent was standing up all by itself. The two friends were ready to begin their camping adventure.

"I'll spread out our blanket to cover the ground," said Molly.

"We need pillows, Molly," said Emmett. "This ground is pretty hard."

In the house, Emmett got his blue fish pillow and
several more large fluffy cushions.

Then Emmett and Molly gathered toys, games, and books for something to do inside the tent.

"Don't we need flashlights, Molly?" asked Emmett. "It's getting sort of dark."

"You're right, Em," said Molly. "And I need my sweater."

Now the tent was bright and cozy, just like inside
Molly and Emmett's house.

"Are you having a good time, Em?" asked Molly.
"No. I'm hungry, and WE FORGOT THE PICNIC
STUFF, Molly!" said Emmett.

Molly and Emmett ran back inside to pack a picnic basket.

They put in sandwich stuff

and fruit and juice and pickles

and cookies for dessert and plenty of tuna.

And a couple of chicken legs, too.

17

"This is really camping, Em," said Molly. "Didn't
I promise you it would be fun?"

"It might be more fun if it weren't raining," said Emmett as a big fat raindrop fell on his head.

"Rain?" cried Molly. "Yikes!"

20

BOOM! There was a big clap of thunder. The sky got very dark, and rain began to fall—*SPLAT, SPLAT, SPLAT*— harder and harder.

"Quick, Em, into the tent!"
said Molly. "I'm getting soaked!"
"We can't get all the way in,
Molly," said Emmett. "We brought
too much stuff!"

"Run for the house, Emmett," cried Molly.
"This isn't fun anymore!"

"I'm way ahead of you, Molly," hollered Emmett,
wringing out his soggy pillow.

"You were right, Emmett," said Molly. "It DID rain. But our pretend tent is just as much fun."

"I think it's MORE fun," said Emmett, sipping his cocoa. "It isn't raining in here."

The two friends agreed. Camping out is for sunny weather. Camping in is for anytime.

27

Planning a Campout

Your supplies

- A tent! If you don't own a real tent, fasten blankets over a line strung between two trees, a clothesline, or another support. A tarp or waterproof sheet spread under the tent will keep ground moisture out.
- Sleeping gear. Even if you won't be spending the night outside, it's fun to curl up in a sleeping bag or nest of blankets and pillows. An air mattress, roll of foam padding, or carpet squares can make a soft surface.
- Flashlights or camping lantern.
- Backpack or duffle bag to carry special stuff such as toys, games, and books.

Daytime activities

• Setting up the campsite is part of the fun! Spread ground cloths, pitch the tent, and spread a picnic blanket.

• Go for a hike and let your imagination create a wilderness wherever you are. A puddle can be a lake, a crack in the sidewalk can be a ravine. Talk about the insects and animals you see.

• Play ring-toss or beanbag/ball-tossing games.

• Lie down, look at clouds, and tell stories about the shapes you see.

• Use dolls and toy animals to act out imaginary camping adventures.

After-dark activities

• Gather together for family time to share songs and stories.

• Play the "song game" to see how many songs you can think of with a certain theme in them such as colors ("Little Red Caboose," "Yellow Submarine," "Lavender's Blue"), weather ("Rain, Rain, Go Away," "You Are My Sunshine"), nursery rhyme characters, or any themes you choose.

• Tell stories. A circular story Emmett loves goes like this: "It was a dark and stormy night, and brigands large and brigands small were seated around the campfire. 'Antonio,' said the captain, 'tell us a story,' and Antonio told as follows. 'It was a dark and stormy night, and brigands large and brigands small were seated around the campfire. 'Antonio,' said the captain, 'tell us a story,' and Antonio told as follows. 'It was a dark and stormy night . . .'" and so on.

• Tell jokes and riddles. If you don't know very many, check for joke books at your public library.

• Look at the stars and point out familiar constellations, or make up your own star pictures and tell stories about them.

• Set up a shadow play. Place a lantern inside the tent and stand between the light and the side of the tent. Use your whole body or try making shadow figures with your hands.

LOOK MOLLY! A FISH!

I DON'T THINK SO, EMMETT.